A GERM

A FIGHT AGAINST RESISTANCE

A GERM'S JOURNEY

A FIGHT AGAINST RESISTANCE

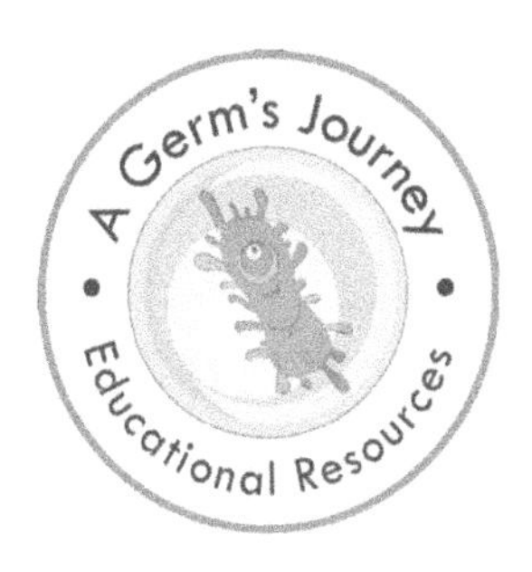

J.W. GLOVER, K. LAIRD
AND S. YOUNIE

ILLUSTRATED BY
SARAH ROBINSON

Matador
9 Priory Business Park,
Wistow Road, Kibworth Beauchamp,
Leicestershire. LE8 0RX
Tel: 0116 279 2299
Email: books@troubador.co.uk
Web: www.troubador.co.uk/matador
Twitter: @matadorbooks

ISBN 9781800464070

British Library Cataloguing in Publication Data.
A catalogue record for this book is available from the British Library.

Printed and bound by CPI Group (UK) Ltd, Croydon, CR0 4YY
Typeset in 12pt Baskerville by Troubador Publishing Ltd, Leicester, UK

Matador is an imprint of Troubador Publishing Ltd

This book is dedicated to all the children around the world and the teachers that educate them.

– The Germ's Journey Team

And to Iris, thank you for always believing in me.
I hope I forever make you proud of the stories I tell.
I do it for you.

– Joe

Acknowledgements

This book wouldn't have been possible if it wasn't for a number of people working so hard to make it happen and offering their unwavering support.

In particular, for inspiring the pathfinder format of the book, we would like to thank Rachel King for her insightful contribution.

We also would like to take the time to thank Ahmed Aboo for the invaluable knowledge that he has provided to the project.

The book would not be the same without the beautiful illustrations created by Sarah Robinson. Her amazing craft has brilliantly brought to life the world and characters that have been imagined for this book, and for that we are incredibly indebted to her.

1

Your hand begins to shake, crumpling the ticket even more than it already has. You haven't dared to let it out of your grip all day – you daren't even think about misplacing it and miss out on going. You can hardly contain yourself, your eyes fixed on the doors eager for them to open. Why won't they open already?

CLUNK

Was that the door? Is it time yet? Your eyes dart towards the doors for the slightest glimmer of light creeping through the crack. What must lie behind the doors?

CLICK

Okay, something must be about to happen. It's been long enough. You've been stood for what seems like an eternity with your heels slowly sinking into the tiled floor. The helpful lady said it was only going to be a couple of minutes when she dropped you off. Maybe it has only been a few minutes, but minutes can seem like a lifetime when you're willing away each and every second just to get this started.

CLUNK

What could be happening behind there? It's clear that something is going on behind the closed doors. Your eyes peer through the gap between the two pieces of metal.

CLUNK CLUNK

Your bum hits the cold floor as you fall backwards startled by the noise.

CLUNK

The noise has begun to get louder now; more fierce, more alive

CLUNK

- and faster.

CLUNK

You try to drag yourself onto your feet, but you buckle again. The room has started to shake just as a large whirring has started to drown out the clunking. The ticket escapes your grip.

You look around to see the room is now tinted with ruby red.

"Attention all crew and personnel!" Your head whips towards the speaker. "The air shuttle is ready for loading. Please make your way outside to the launch pad now."

Finally. This is the moment you've been waiting for ever since you laid your eyes on that letter at your front door. The honour! You've been selected above thousands of other applicants to get this position. A chance to experience more out of life; a chance to make a difference for everyone; a chance to be part of the team combatting antibiotic resistance. Today will be your first day as a trainee agent in the Anti-Bio Squad.

The metal doors slide open. You take in the fresh air. Without you realising, your foot has made the first step towards the aircraft, almost as if it's being pulled that way. You're ready.

2

The door to the plane flings open in an upwards direction and a set of stairs slide down to your feet inviting you on. Climbing the stairs, you look to your right to see the initials 'ABS' between the plane's two sets of wings. The 'Anti-Bio Squad'. This is really happening.

You turn down the aisle as you enter the plane. It's like no plane you've encountered before. Pairs of seats facing each other, with a brown table in between. It is more reminiscent of a train than anything else. Each table has a monitor in the middle of it, probably to display missions on. You take your place on a seat of four in the middle of the plane – not the first face at the front that everyone will see, but not hidden away at the back. You've picked the ideal spot to take in everything that is going to happen.

You start to hear muffled voices slowly make their way up the runway and onto the plane. They have probably made this journey time and time before and so do not have that same buzz to get to the aircraft. Or it may seem that you were more under control by the excitement that you rushed onto the aircraft slightly quicker than you intended. Either way, you were the first to board and your heroes would become your colleagues as soon as their feet step onto the aircraft. You crane your neck forward trying to pull the first face onto the plane with your vision.

The voices patter their way onto the steps of the plane from faint whispers to fully understandable words and sentences. Each step on the stairway is like a volume button on the remote, becoming louder and louder. You begin to feel the leather under you become slippery as you continue to lock your eyes onto the doorway.

Your eyes nearly fall out of their sockets as the first face finally emerges into sight, followed by more voices and faces. It is not long until it becomes a steady stream of faces, all the bright and brave boys and girls, the coolest teens that you have ever looked up to – both figuratively and now, finally, physically. Everyone knows anything and everything about the squad. Their every move is watched and reported because they mean so much to the world. They are true heroes, let alone celebrities. They are the ones that help to keep everyone safe from bacterial danger. Without them, the world would not be the place it is. The world would not be as safe and healthy as it is. Each person that passes you puts another muscle in your face to work to add to your already beaming smile. The Anti-Bio Squad are here!

The Anti-Bio Squad members pass you by, taking their own seats on the plane. None of them really give you much attention but your mind begins to go into overdrive, picturing the poster pinned to your wall back home and ticking each member off as you see them. They are all here. And you are here with them.

"Hey there!" You turn your head to the direction of the voice. "Nice to meet you. The name is Max." Like you needed to be told. He is just as he appears in your poster. A tall, slim teen that stands bold and brave to any obstacle put in front of him. His dark hair is in tight curls poking out of his baseball cap that he is wearing backwards – although you're used to seeing him with a short afro. His uniform matches his dark and mysterious aura, a mixture of greys and blacks with the red trim detailing along his shirt is the only colour to stand out. He has the circular Anti-Bio Squad logo on his chest, although you noticed that there seems to be a mixture of different shapes on everyone's uniform. Something about Max made him appear to always be smiling,

even in some of the tougher situations that have been reported on TV. He just has a calming nature around him. His coolness oozing out. Max, and the whole Anti-Bio Squad, are as great as superheroes. "I hate to say this to you but you're kinda in my seat."

Oh no.

You had every intention to do all you could to fit in and be a proper member of the squad and be accepted, not to stand out from the start and upset them – especially over something so small. You gaze down at the armrest and it indeed says, 'Agent Maximus Addison'.

"Max, it's their first day, leave them alone." The voice joins the conversation before the face does. "He is just joking around. He is always like this. He doesn't need to sit there – do you, Max?" It was Georgie, another hero of the Anti-Bio Squad. She is known to be a fiery member in the squad. She is no pushover to the baddy bacteria; she can more than hold her own. Georgie always gives her all and gets right into the thick of the action and yet still is able to keep her blonde ponytail intact. Her uniform is similar to Max's except with a blue trim detail and her squad logo being an upside-down triangle.

"Yeah, I'm kidding, honest. You'll learn that I like to have a joke around here, it's always good to keep a bit

of humour when you do what we do. Fighting germs all day, every day, can get to you after so long so there's no harm in a bit of playful banter. I hope you don't mind?"

You didn't mind at all if it meant you would be hanging around with the likes of Max and Georgie.

"So, you must be the trainee that D.O.C was telling us about. He has told us a lot about you, so we are expecting big things." Georgie gives you a playful wink. Had the Anti-Bio Squad really been talking about you? You?!

"I bet you must be a mix bag of nerves and excitement. Don't worry, I was the same when I started. We will look after you, won't we Max?" Georgie gives a glare at Max, trying to influence his answer.

"Of course! You're in safe hands here. You stick with us and you will be just fine. Now, I don't know what you know about us but there's more to us than what's shown on TV. There's a lot of work and effort that goes on behind the scenes. A lot of hard, long hours so I hope you're ready for it, Newbie, because…"

"Oh, you're not doing the Newbie nickname again, are you?" Georgie cut Max off, snapping at the comment he made.

"Well yeah, everyone is a Newbie when they start. And they will stay a Newbie until they prove themselves as a member of the team. And…" pausing for a second, Max appeared to have a look of embarrassment on his face. "And, I'm not the best at learning names. So, I guess you're going to be Newbie until I remember your name."

You feel the plane has started to move and begin its take-off process. You shuffle in your seat, the realisation hitting you that this is really happening. You are making your dream a reality. There is no turning back now, you are on the plane and on your way to incredible things. The plane thrusts forward and starts to rise up into the air.

"Are you okay there?" Max says smiling at you before looking in Georgie's direction. "This is just a standard take-off, just like any other plane. But I'm not sure you noticed when you were getting on, this isn't exactly a normal plane. If you didn't enjoy the take-off then I'm pretty sure you're not going to enjoy this next bit."

Your face morphs into a look of confusion and worry. All of a sudden, the plane hurtles up and up and up. The further up the plane goes the further you seem to merge into the seat. You manage to roll your head to the side. Peeling your eyes open to get a glimpse of your surroundings, you catch the sky through the window turn from a blue painting to an almost blank white canvas. The plane begins to shudder as it reaches top speed. You're not sure how much more of this you can take. You close your eyes to try and draw in what little strength remains in your body and – everything levels out.

You watch the plane burst out of the white into almost a golden blue. The plane has eased off in both speed and the angle of the flight. You kid yourself into thinking that you're back to some kind of normality and then, there it is.

"There you go. That floating island over there is The Lab. And that's our home." Max's hand on your shoulder fails to break your gaze outside.

You had heard about it, but you always thought it would be lies or an exaggerated rumour. How could you possibly have an island floating in the air above the world? Yet, here it is. A great white square building stands in the centre of four tall towers, one at each corner. The building pokes in front of a vast forest of trees, apart from a clearway that reveals cliffsides and even a waterfall to one side. It is a paradise island.

"What do you think to it?" Georgie asks with a smile in one corner of her mouth, seemingly knowing what your response will be.

Your hand thrusts the sick bag under your mouth.

"Yeah, I thought the exact same too on my first time!" Max chuckles to Georgie. "You'll be just fine, don't you worry. Just maybe give it a few minutes!"

3

The most pristine white building you have ever seen stands grand and mighty in front of you. From the palm trees surrounding the building to the marble steps leading up to the front door, everything about this place seems majestic. You can't help but allow yourself to be lost in awe of it all.

"Welcome to The Lab. Our little base in the sky." Max grins, seemingly enjoying your amazement.

"Why don't you follow us, and we will show you around the place." Georgie starts the walk up the steps with Max following closely behind. You stand for another breath, just taking in the scenery of it all. You hope that any second you will come to terms in your mind that this is all real, but you still feel like your head is lost in the clouds: except you really are in the clouds. You float up the steps to catch up with both of them.

Two enormous glass doors slide apart to allow the three of you to walk through. You enter a giant lobby, full of people all in their own worlds and rushing over the black and white chequered marble flooring. In the centre of the room a great golden statue shows three individuals standing in an action pose. You get close enough to see a plaque declaring that they were the three founding members of the Anti-Bio Squad. At the back of the room, a grey stone desk spans nearly across the whole of the back room, the longest side of the wall. You are careful to not bump into anyone as everyone appears so intent on carrying on with their important business. However, you do get in the way of a few as your vision gets distracted by the glass skylight above your head.

Your focus switches down and you catch Max and Georgie ahead, walking off without you, about to follow one of the two corridors leading away from the lobby. You rush – worried that you will be left behind and be lost in such a large place.

Catching up with them, your mind wanders once more. The corridor is just as spectacular as the front of the building. The corridor continues and is now accessorised with busts of famous agents that once wore the uniform and fought for the safety of the people. You dare to dream of one day having such a successful time with the squad that you are also honoured in the same way. You start to think about the number of stories that each face must have, the number of missions each must have accomplished, the achievements they have gained, it only adds to the excitement that's already bubbling away inside.

The corridor goes on and on, appearing almost endless. The busts have now been replaced with a variety of different plants in overly large pots. Each pot sits beside a door on the corridor walls. The doors have a small black plaque attached at eye level saying names like 'Interview Room 1', 'Meeting Room 3', 'Admin Office' along with others. Rooms are opposite each other and continue all the way up to the next great room.

A set of glass sliding doors invite you into an almighty headquarters, even larger than the lobby before. Everywhere you look, there are computers with teams of people surrounding them, working away. Individuals are also looking at, and analysing information, on monitors and TV screens of a size that you've never come across before. Along the edges of the room in blocks are desks of control panels and buttons, again with more workers studying them with extra attention and care. Just like before, there is a glass skylight above your head.

"This is The Lab. Our main headquarters, good old HQ. All the information we get goes through here. Nothing happens without these guys knowing about it. We wouldn't be able to do the job we do without them." It is clear that Georgie has a great appreciation for all the work that takes place in this room.

"This is where D.O.C. said he would meet us, right?" Max seeming impatient checking the watch on his wrist.

"Yeah, I'm sure he will be here in a few minutes. He's like our boss, by the way. He is in charge of all the operations and the squad, everything goes through him. In fact, that's his title 'Director of Operations and Control'."

"But we just call him D.O.C. because it's so much easier, and I think it suits him well." A puzzled look crosses Max's face. "To be honest, I don't actually know what D.O.C.'s real name is. I don't think anyone knows. I suppose nobody bothered to ask".

"More like everyone is too scared to ask!" Georgie chuckles to herself, before Max joins in. However, their words do little to put you at ease about meeting D.O.C.

A crackle is heard over the speaker system in the room. It is followed by a piercing alarm.

"Attention agents! Incoming message from the D.O.C." You flick your head around trying to locate the speaker that the sound is coming from. The screens across the entire side wall flicker into life, forming one grand image for a video call.

"Good morning agents". A deep husky voice is heard from the speaker.

"Good morning D.O.C." Both Max and Georgie deliver a greeting as if they were back at school doing the register for a teacher. The two are both facing the screens, now showing the image of an older man, older than your dad but not quite at the same stage as your grandfather. He appears to be more similar to a professor than a doctor, someone you'd expect to wear a tweed jacket. He wears a pristine white shirt, a harness which his badge is attached to, with a bowtie. His top lip is hidden by a thick bushy moustache. His slicked back hair reveals his receding hairline the colour of black, grey, and white. It is clear, however, that the little black hair he has left is on the transition to being grey and white also.

"I see you both have met and are looking after our new trainee. Excellent. Welcome aboard to the team. You are in safe hands don't you fret." His moustache and eyebrows appearing very animated on the screen as if they are being controlled like a puppet on strings. “This has worked out quite nicely actually. If you two don’t mind, would you stay with our new trainee and be the guiding company until they are all settled in?”

“Of course, D.O.C. anything you need. In fact, I quite like Newbie.” Your cheeks begin to blush because of Max’s flattering remark.

“Newbie? Hoh, oh Max, you, honestly!” The nickname amuses D.O.C. so that he scoffs and snorts. “Very well, we will keep Newbie with you two. Now, I should let you know that you probably won’t work with both of them for the whole time. We work in speciality teams here, just so that we can maximise our strengths in each specific area. This is why Max and Georgie, here, are both wearing uniform with slightly different badges embroidered on them. Each logo signifies the antibiotic medicine that they are trained in and look after: Max being the lead agent of our team utilising penicillin; and Georgie heading up our ciprofloxacin division. This means that a mission will only require one agent’s team and one antibiotic type for treatment at a time, or we may realise the mission doesn’t need any antibiotics to be used at all. It is this that makes it your job as a team to investigate the condition that the patient has and what

action should be taken – if at all. You then administer the antibiotic to the patient with these little beauties." D.O.C. pulls out a remote from his pocket and points it towards the big screen displaying a super soaker like weapon.

"These are the Capsule Cannons, our best ally in the bacteria battlefield that we find ourselves in. Each cannon contains the antibiotic that is specifically required for your mission. Equally, the Capsule Cannon is an instrument used to deploy tablets, capsules, or whatever is required for the specific case. We use the cannons to rapidly disperse the antibiotics effectively and efficiently in the mouth, down the throat, and into the stomach where it can enter the bloodstream. The cannon will fire out the correct dosage to the patient and we calculate the correct number of recurring visits and dosages to destroy the bacteria, and if we've done our job well, then the patient will be right as rain again. If we haven't, then it isn't too much to say the consequences are huge. If we wrongly identify the illness and treat bacteria that turns out to be just a virus then we risk giving the bacteria more power. The bacteria will gain resistance to our antibiotics, making them stronger and then we will no longer be able to fight the bacteria in that child and make them better. But let's just make sure that this doesn't happen, and it doesn't come to that."

You stand there rooted to the spot in amazement, trying to take in the information you have just received.

"Now that's been sorted, let's put Newbie straight to work. We've had reports come in of an illness crime. The patient is Jacob, age 9, from the Midlands in the UK. He has come down with a blocked nose, sore throat, and just generally feeling quite tired – sounds quite normal really and indeed some of HQ think it's nothing. Just the standard virus causing a common cold. But there are some who reckon it sounds a little more serious. Either way, we need to find out and treat this boy and I want you three to go down there to figure this one out."

Wow, your first mission already. This is not something you expected at all. You were just over the moon to be here and would be quite happy to be sorting files behind a desk at first. But this is huge to be sent out into the field without any training to go on. They must have really liked your application. At least you won't have to make any big decisions though just yet.

"Oh, and kid, I want you to take the lead on this one. When you guys get down there, it's your call what action to take. It's time to show us what you've got. Don't mess up!" The screen turns to black. Great.

Already you are feeling your skin burn up with the

pressure put on you by the D.O.C. How can he trust you with so much already? How can this be all on your shoulders? What's going to happen if you mess up? You start to feel the sickly knot in your stomach again but this time there's no plane involved.

"Hey, don't worry you've got this." Your eyes must have given away your worry to Max.

"Yeah, it will be okay. You wouldn't be here if they didn't think you could handle it." You want to believe Georgie, but you start to wonder whether this has all been a mistake. You have never even come across anything close to this.

"Listen, you will be going down with us and our AAs." You look back a little blank at the expression but don't want to ask any questions as you feel as though you should already know the answer. "We will be there the whole time, and we will give you all the help you need. So just relax and enjoy the whole experience. But make the right choice – the D.O.C. hates mistakes and having to put them right. So, no pressure really. Anyway, let's get suited up and do this thing!"

You follow Max and Georgie through a set of automatic sliding doors to a locker room full of lockers, uniforms, and equipment.

"Here, put this on." Max smirks to you. Looking

down you see no logo on the shirt and instead the word "TRAINEE" in a large font. Well it was true. You only hope that any microbe villain you encounter will see the label and take things easy on you rather than use it as a target. "Come on, we need to pick up our AA's. I can't wait for you to meet Penny". Of course, how could you forget – AA as in 'Animal Assistant'.

You venture into another room to the left; it is filled with a selection of the world's creatures. From apes to pigs, from lions to horses, it seems as if every animal is in this room. However, you notice there is no chaos. All the animals are getting along and going about their day and their duties like any human would.

"It's incredible, right?" Max seemed as in awe as you are.

"All the animals you see here have been rescued." Georgie, seemingly being able to read your confusion in the situation. "One way or another these animals were in some sort of danger or neglect. And then they were rescued and came to us. Through a bit of training and a lot of love, they became the model beings that they are now. They are the true heroes of the squad."

"And here are ours now. Come here, girl. Who's a good girl? Aw I missed you Penny. Uh, oh, sorry about that it's been a while since I saw her."

A medium sized dalmatian and a large black cat trot over to your group. They both seemed bright-eyed and excited to not only be there but also to greet their partners and you, the new recruit. Max too appears just as excited, rubbing and petting Penny's head as he rubs her belly. "The amazing thing is that each agent gets paired with the animal that perfectly fits their needs and personality and then they will become their partner on missions. And believe me, Penny has saved my bacon more times than I can remember when we are out in the field. Hey, you see their collar and their harness? They have special technology in them that reads their mind and sends it to our headpiece so that they can communicate with us. Mad right?" This whole thing is so mad that things are starting to become believable to you.

Georgie turns to you with the black cat cradled in her arms. "When you guys are about finished, you can follow me and Eddie onto the plane – thank you."

You all board the plane, a smaller aircraft than the big shuttle you were in before but identical in design. Only this time you find yourself in the cockpit. The room is a panorama of buttons, gadgets, and gizmos that all must have their own special use. Max takes the primary seat in front of the main bulk of controls. You take the padded seat to his right as Georgie takes the one to the left. Turning your head, you catch Penny and Eddie in the corner strapping themselves into their own special seats.

You feel Georgie's hand reaching across and gently tapping you on the arm. "I strongly advise you to buckle yourself in tightly. Especially as this is your first time."

The panic nearly bursts out of your eyes. Your fingers scrabble around trying to find your belt to attach to the buckle. You are not going to risk a repeat of last time. The buckle barely makes the connection in time.

CLICK … *WHOOSH*

The jet engines roar into life. Before you realise it, you are hurtling out of the hangar. Off the runway. Off the island. The plane fires like a canon back down to Earth. Your fingernails cling to the seat as you to try anything to control yourself. The experience is worse than the one before. You close your eyes as if to will it all to stop.

But the realisation hits that you have the unique chance to see the world in a way that many can only dream of. You peel your eyes apart to stare out of the windshield, the big bay window in the front of the cockpit. A beautiful enormous orb of blues and greens lies in front of you, with sprinklings of white to decorate.

For a moment, you are released from the pressure of the plane.

The pressure builds once more as the globe rushes closer and closer to you. Your picture of the world becomes focused to a continent, then a single country, a region, a city. Everything is zooming in at such a great speed, you feel your breath beginning to panic. Looking at Max and Georgie's faces of cool, calm, collection they seem to be more than happy and have no intentions of slowing down.

You flick back to the window. It's a town now, a neighbourhood, a street. A boy comes into view. You are heading straight towards him! You begin to see him clearly. It is the boy Jacob that the mission is focused around. But you are still heading towards him. You can see his face clearly now, his smile focused down towards the action figure in his hand. He is completely unaware of the crash that is bound to happen at any moment now. You are flying head-on into a poor 9-year-old boy. He opens his mouth to smile, you see his ginormous teeth rise above the ship. Ginormous teeth above the ship?

The plane slows down to land on the landing strip on the tongue. Max turns to you, before quickly turning away to grab and pass you another sick bag.

4

You follow the gang out of the plane, somewhat still shaken from the experience. Your gaze wanders around to take in the surroundings. If it wasn't for knowing the journey you took to get here, you would be forgiven for believing you were in a cave. Droplets fall from the roof above and the moist ground made for a dark damp setting.

"How are you feeling after that one then?" Max chuckles after patting you on the back. "And you thought getting to The Lab was a bumpy ride! Anyway, no time to waste. We are here now, inside your first body on your very first mission. Doesn't quite seem real, does it? I can promise you though, we are inside the mouth of a human boy. So maybe be careful where you step, don't want to be losing you just yet!" You feel the hot redness fill your cheeks once again.

"Stop it Max, this is scary enough as it is without

you winding things up and making it worse. Don't you remember what it was like on your first mission?" Like a schoolboy that's just been told off, Max can only shrug his shoulders in response. "Now let's start, shall we? Why don't you take Newbie around with you on your sweep of the area, so you can go through everything that needs to be checked? I'm going to take Eddie and do a quick look around myself."

"Good idea. Come on, Newbie. Let's split up and look for clues! Well, germs really but it doesn't quite sound as good."

You walk with Max and Penny over to the side of the cave. You want to closely examine the sides of the mouth for anything out of the ordinary and so you climb onto a molar boulder to get a better view. Your hand slips on the wet tooth and lands in a pile of food debris between two teeth.

"I am not going to lie to you, the thought of being inside a human's mouth is so disgusting at the start. It really is. But you get used to it, you have to. It's our job at the end of the day." How Max can keep doing his job is a mystery to you? He must have been doing this for a while to be used to all this gunk.

From the better height, you shine your torch along the sides of the mouth. The light illuminates more than just the walls, as the pinkness in front of you tells you that you're definitely not in a cave. Your light sweeps left to right, and top to bottom, but you spot nothing unusual about this part of the mouth.

"This is the thing." Switching his torch off, Max turns to your direction. "We are made out to be these great heroes who are constantly fighting to keep everyone healthy but the majority of cases we look into end up with us not taking any action. They are either false calls, you know, there's nothing really going on, or it's something small – a virus like the common cold. Either way, there's not anything we can do to help. We've still got to go down and check though because on the odd occasion there is something more serious going on. You definitely don't want to be there if D.O.C. finds out you missed one of the bacteria villains." You nod your head to agree, but also still too scared to fully talk to him. "Well there really isn't anything going on here. Let's check out the back of the throat and if there's still nothing then we will call it a day and head back to The Lab. I'm sorry it's not been the most exciting case so far." You are quite relieved inside.

Approaching the back of the throat it becomes quite clear to you that there is at least a sign of bacteria or virus being here. Traces of gunky sludge lines the back of the throat, like a piece of slime stuck to your hand.

"Ah, well isn't this lovely for you. Somebody has definitely been here and committed a germ attack on this boy. No surprise that whoever did this is hiding right now. What tends to happen is that they catch wind of us coming down to investigate and then they go into hiding for a while." Spitting out his words, Max seems quite frustrated by this. "There's a fair bit of mucus lining the throat but not too much to suggest a bacterial infection just yet." He scoops a handful of the gunk off the throat. "And they have made the throat fairly red and sore. It's probably just the work of the Rhinos and their virus again, which would be no biggie, or we've just missed them, and this is the very early stages of the infection. Here, take a look at the file we have on the Rhinos." A tablet device is shoved in your hand as Max's attention switches to the front of the mouth. "How's it going with you, Georgie?"

Georgie wanders over from the other side of the mouth. "Yeah, there's not a lot going on from what I saw. I did get an alert from D.O.C. of another case that's come up and he wants me to take a look at. It's clear that this isn't going to need ciprofloxacin for treatment of bacteria so I'm gonna head straight out now and I'll take one of the escape pods. I trust that you two have everything covered here."

"Yeah, I think you're right. No worries, G. Best of luck with yours. Catch you later." Georgie waves you both goodbye and takes quick strides to the plane with Eddie following at her heels.

"Well, I think we are about done here too. If it is the Rhinos, which is what it looks like to be honest, then there's really nothing we can do. They're an absolute nuisance but at least they will be gone and moved on in a few days. We can still try to grab the chief and ruffle him up though to see if we can get them to clear off any quicker."

You trust Max's assessment of the situation and both turn in the direction of the plane. You barely take a stride before you catch Penny circling a spot near the back of the tongue, head locked on something higher up.

"Maximus, Maximus! Look Maximus."

A slightly embarrassed chuckle escapes Max's mouth. "Max is short for Maximus. Umm, what is it girl? What have you spotted?"

"Nose. Nose. Dripping from the nose."

Both you and Max tilt your heads up the throat and shine torches to try and shed more light onto the situation. It isn't a lot, but a couple of very dark green mucus droplets are falling down from the nasal cavity and a few white pussy spots on the tonsils can be seen.

"Well, this does change things slightly. Good spot, Pen! You'll be getting a treat back at the base." Max cups Penny's face between his fingers from the top of her head to under her ears.

"This may still be the Rhinos causing havoc, they do like to cause a lot of mucus. But very dark green may be a sign of something else. Which means, there is a chance that this is the work of Empress Strepto and her Coccus Clan." Max once more passes you the tablet to read through the file on *Streptococcus* bacteria which causes bacterial tonsillitis. "If it is the work of Empress Strepto, then we do have some action to take. We will need to head back to The Lab, call it into D.O.C, and then get our supplies to head back here and deal with this."

You purse your lips to deliver your response.

"But it needs to be the right decision. The wrong call can mean this poor boy not being treated properly and getting sicker. That, or Empress Strepto becoming resistant to our antibiotic weapons because we give the wrong antibiotics. Or we give them for the wrong length of time, which would mean we won't be able to help Jacob in the future when he does need treatment, because the antibiotics won't work as well. It all can be a waste of supplies, a waste of effort, and a waste of time." For once, Max is not showing his smiling side as he normally would. "So, Newbie, you have the fact file, the Rhinos or Empress Strepto, what's it going to be?"

It's your decision as to which suspect to pursue in the case. Turn to the next two pages to read the case files and decide which path to take.

If you think this was the work of Empress Strepto, then turn to page 79.

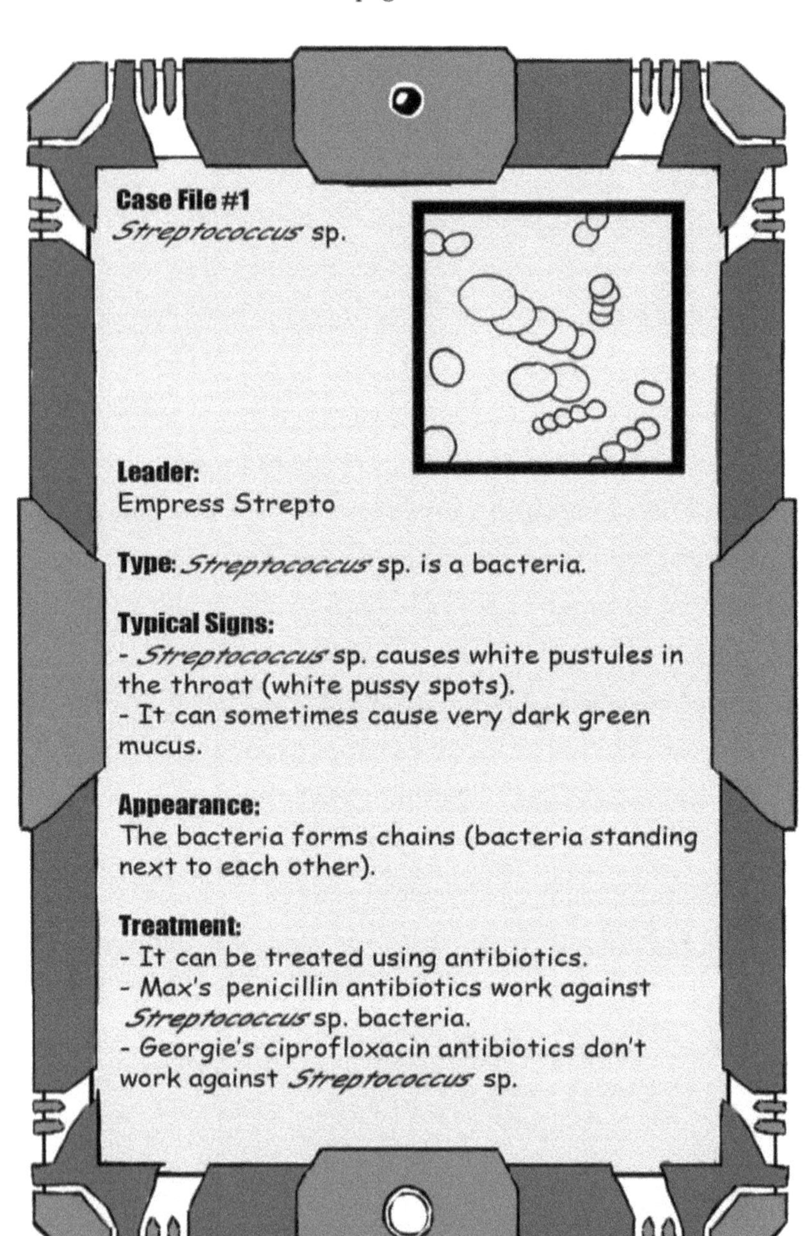

Or, if you think this looks more like the doing of the Rhinos, then turn to page 42.

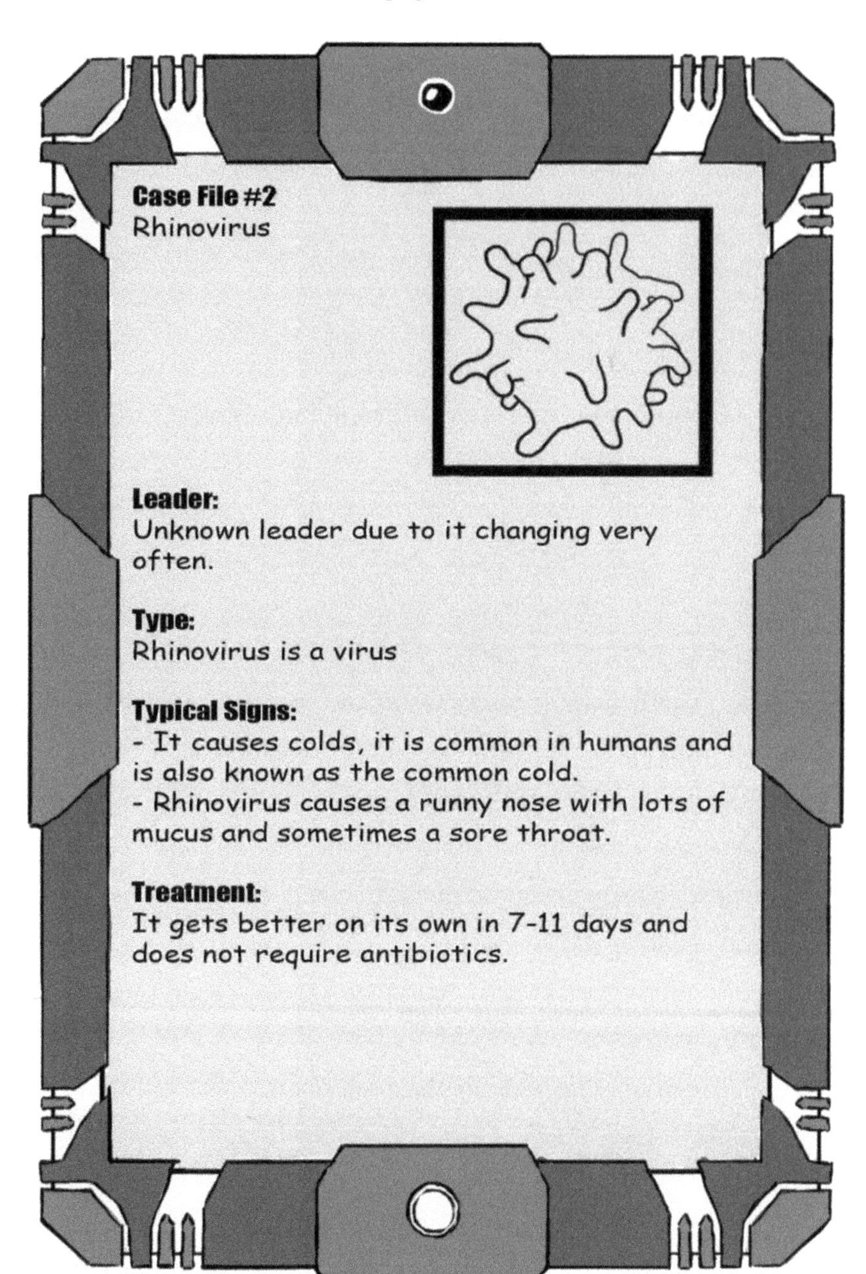

7a

Your finger glides over the 'Send Help?' button to reply to Georgie. You apologise to her for not sending the help but explain your decision; that you didn't think it was the right thing because the penicillin antibiotics only work against certain bacteria and may cause resistance in the bacteria that Georgie is fighting, and you just wanted to follow the orders of D.O.C and Max. You half close your eyes as you send the message as if that will take away any of the responsibility for making the decision. You then close the tablet and just hold it for a few minutes. The room makes a couple of turns whilst you are stood there. In one deep breath, the room steadies itself.

You hear the familiar echoing of footsteps running up the corridor.

"Newbie! They are loading the plane. We need to get moving right now. Come on, follow me." Here you go again. He grabs the tablet from your hand and then grabs your other hand dragging you up the corridor with him.

There's a frantic buzz bouncing its way between everyone on the plane. You are sat with Max in the cockpit as before but now joining you in the main compartment of the plane are five operatives.

"It's always easier having a little helping hand in situations like this. We really do go into it blind; we have no idea how many of Strepto's clan is going to be there, so we need the operatives as back up. We will still use the same dosage of penicillin against the *Streptococcus*, we just spread it out amongst us all. We have to make sure we follow the right dosage plan, so regular doses 4 times a day for the next 7 days. And we ALWAYS have to make sure we use every last bit up. We can't allow Empress Strepto to grow resistant to the treatment by messing up the dosage, otherwise we will be left with nothing to fight her off with. We can't risk the health of children, because she will not stop unless we stop her. This is why getting today right is so important. The first treatment is always the hardest – the toughest battle. How it's going to work is that we are going to be here for this initial big fight but hopefully we will do our job right today, and we can leave the back-up to deal with the other dosages in shifts."

You turn away from Max, looking out to the empty sky outside the window. You hope that your eyes don't give away about how nervous you are for your first battle. It's the right thing, it needs to be done and this is exactly what you signed up for, but these thoughts don't do anything to settle the butterflies in your stomach.

"Okay, I'm just going to double-check the dosages again, make sure we've got it right. The last thing we want is to be out there, mid-battle and suddenly realise that we don't have enough and need more and…" Your attention switches back to Max. Whatever it is that he is looking at on the tablet has stopped him right in his tracks. Something must have happened. "Newbie. Did you get a message from Georgie asking to share tablets with her? Because there's a request on here from today."

In the frantic rush boarding the plane and setting off you had completely forgotten to update Max on Georgie's message. Your whole body becomes heavy with guilt.

"Hey, don't look like that. I don't get why you look so worried. You made the right call!" A huge sigh forces its way out from between your lips, and you suddenly feel ten stone lighter. Max, seemingly noticing your change in state, lets out one of his trademark smiles. "Don't worry, I knew all about it all along." You raise an eyebrow in Max's direction. "It was all an act; Georgie didn't really need your help. She was putting it on so that D.O.C. could test you, he does it to everyone. That was a toughie though, being put under that kind of pressure. On your own too. It takes a big character to make a big decision like that." He beams a smile once more. "I'm excited now to see what you have to offer in the field. You're definitely proving that D.O.C. was right to invite you to train with the Anti-Bio Squad, good job!"

Turn to page 53 to continue to the next stage of the case.

5a

A bead of sweat drips down from your brow. You have never experienced a heat like it, especially to sweep over you in such a short period of time. You take your eyes away from the tablet to gaze up at Max. His eyes are not offering the answer you were hoping for. They just wait, expecting an answer. Surely, they wouldn't leave such an enormous decision to a trainee rookie like yourself. There's too much on the line for you to be allowed to be wrong. Max did say that there wasn't as much mucus as there can be and so he thought it was the Rhino gang and their virus. You decide to take Max's first impression and choose to go after the Rhino gang.

"Okay, if that's your choice then let's do this. We will see if we can track down the Rhino boss, whoever it is at the moment."

No sooner had the words left Max's mouth, a slightly muffled groan is heard from behind a tooth on the other side of the mouth that you had checked out earlier. Turning to Max, he greets your look with the same confused expression. Without a word being uttered, you both start the cautious walk to the source of the noise.

You approach the tooth where the noise sounded like it came from. You feel Max's arm come across your chest holding you back. He lifts his finger to his lips, before signalling to you to wait. He edges forward halfway over the tooth. He turns to you; his trademark smile has returned. Suddenly, in one swift motion he flings himself over the tooth and pulls a creature back over with him. A small goblin like creature emerges, trapped in Max's grip.

"Look what we have here. It just so happens the Rhinos are hiding like the cowards they are. And we've only gone and caught us the head horn himself." The Rhino boss is the figure of a sweaty blob. His grey face is smothered in a grease like liquid, and you notice it dripping onto a scruffy oversized suit. "Right, you can come with us back to The Lab. Come on. We will take you for questioning."

*

You stand next to Max in front of the glass side of a

one-way mirror. Through the glass, a frustrated figure sits alone at a table in one of the many interview rooms at The Lab. The Rhino boss' eyes dart around the room impatiently, letting out a brief snort every once in a while.

"I'm going to take the lead on this one, Newbie. Mainly because these guys have a reputation of not being the brightest bunch. They are literally all called Ryan and if anything happens to the head then they just put another one in the exact same suit. This is one of the reasons why it's so difficult to deal with them. But come on, I'll do most of the talking."

The pair of you walk round into the questioning room, Max leading in front of you. Max's back is straight, and shoulders arched back, an intimidating stance. You feel compelled to try to copy him.

"So, Ryan the Rhino boss is it?" Max turns to you with a cheeky grin and a wink.

"No." The Rhino splutters out. "He was the old boss from a couple of weeks ago."

"Alright." Both you and Max are taken aback from the response, not expecting there to have been a change. "Well, is your name Ryan?"

"Yes". The pair of you exchange confused looks once again.

"Right. And are you the boss of the Rhino gang?"

"Yes". A third look is exchanged. This time, Max's eyes roll as does his patience.

"So… doesn't that make you the Rhino boss?" A few seconds pass by of nothing. Leaning forward, Ryan prepares a response before a fly distracts him. "Ryan!"

"Huh, oh yeah, yeah I guess it does make me Ryan the Rhino boss!" He chuckles and scoffs, a green snot bubble forming from a nostril. It balloons in size for a second before he scoffs once more and sniffs it back inside. "I guess I am yeah. Well, you see there's been a few of us. And we've been the same really. But we are different…" Max's expression becomes stern as his last bit of patience disappears.

"RYAN! We do not have the time for family histories." Slamming the file to the desk. "Right now, there's a boy that's not well and it's our job to make him better. Now are you going to get your boys and quietly move on so he can get better sooner, or am I going to make sure he gets some Calpol and wash you lot out? We will never wipe you all out, but I am sure we can bring a few of you down!" Both you and Ryan stand there startled by Max's fighting talk.

"No. Please don't do that!"

"Well, you know the drill, it's time for your guys to

get out and go." You have never seen such an intense stare as the one that Max is locking onto Ryan right now.

"No, I mean, don't do all of that because it weren't us. Like, yeah there's a few of us there and we did a little bit of messing around. But the worst of it weren't us. We got muscled out by this bigger group. Once they started, we just let them take over, no way were we gonna mess with them, you know." You swap a look with Max one final time, but more concerned than any one before.

"It wasn't you? Well if it wasn't you, then that means..."

"ALERT! ATTENTION ALL AGENTS! INCOMING MESSAGE FROM THE D.O.C." The message rings out across the whole base. Instinctively, you and Max run out of the room and down the corridors in quick time to reach the centre hub of the base. The screen flickers into life just as you both arrive there.

"What on Earth has gone on? I sent you down to check on that boy's case. I get word that he's got strep throat and you are here talking to a Rhino? Explain yourselves!" It appears this was the wrong side of D.O.C. that Max was talking of about earlier.

"It wasn't Newbie's fault, D.O.C. It was a weird one, I wasn't even sure. I should have given more guidance, I'm sorry."

"I don't care who's fault it is, I just want it fixing now! But it's not a good start Newbie. Now do better." The screen fades to black once more.

"I'm sorry, I tried to help. I wasn't sure, I did have a hunch it might have been Strepto's work, but I wanted you to make your own call. We can put this right though, don't worry." Max's arm pulls your shoulder in for a sideward hug.

Turn to page 74 to find out what's next in the investigation.

9b

You stand with your foot hovering over the step on the plane. You take the first step but as soon as you do your mind is flooded with the lessons taught to you by D.O.C. and Max. Then finally, you think about Jacob who you're inside of right now. You owe it to him to help him feel the best that he can and to get rid of the bacteria that are making him ill. You drag yourself away from the step and sprint to the back of the throat. Holding the trigger down, you unload the entire Capsule Cannon down Jacob's throat. You pull the trigger a further couple of times to ensure that it is empty before you return to the plane as quickly as possible.

Entering the plane, you receive a few jeers from those on the plane. They are all exhausted and apparently very anxious to get back to The Lab.

"What took you so long Newbie? I thought we had finished?" Max quizzed you for your absence. You feel compelled to tell him the honest truth about the Capsule Cannon.

"Oh nice! Yeah good call. Nice work, Newbie. Come on, home time."

*

Landing back at the base, you can't help but to reflect on the events of today. You mind boggles trying to understand how it all happened in such a short period of time. So many crazy things that you never considered would possibly happen to you have all come in one day.

"It's crazy right? I'd say it's not always like this. But then I would be lying!" Max walks away sniggering to himself. You're not sure whether it is out of nerves or of exhaustion, but you realise that you are chuckling too. Shaking your head, you follow in the direction of Max to catch up with him.

Max reaches the doors to the control room ahead of you but pauses just before entering. He looks over to you as you approach then stops you. Without saying a word, his trademark cheeky grin appears across his face. He practically pushes you into a control room full of squad members who are busy working. They sense somebody entering the room and turn to greet the new face. Upon realising the face belonged to you, a chorus of applause breaks out across the entire room.

"This is all for you. This is down to your incredible hard work today. Enjoy it. Take it all in." Max allows another chuckle to escape. "Just don't expect it every time!"

The room take it in turns to approach you and to congratulate you on your first mission. Many of the workers you haven't met yet, but they are all more than keen to introduce themselves properly and find out a little bit about you. You notice time beginning to slow at the end of all the greetings. It is only now that you really start to realise that you've done it. You've accomplished your mission. A glow of pride travels over your whole body.

The group of workers continue their praise for you. You begin to feel like a hero being welcomed home from a great war. Then you notice the crowd start to split in the middle. Walking through the split is a tall strong man in a tweed jacket. It's the D.O.C. in the living breathing flesh.

"Good work Newbie!" He outstretches his hand and vigorously shakes it when yours meets his. His firm grip made his words feel all the more sincere. "You've really done us proud. Considering this was your very first mission, and we really threw you into the deep end, I couldn't be more pleased."

You feel two hands on both of your shoulders followed by an embracing hug from both sides. Max and Georgie are there for their turn to shower you with praise.

"Congratulations! I knew as soon as we met that you could do it. I really am so pleased." Somehow, Georgie appears just as pleased about the mission's success as you are.

"Honestly, you were amazing today. You've done so, so well. I am excited to work with you again on more missions, agent". Stepping away, Max delivers one last cheeky grin, but this time accompanied with a playful wink. The D.O.C. moves forward once more to fill Max's place.

"Yes, well all that remains to be said is that everyone really is so pleased with your work that we have decided that this is the end of your trainee programme. And now, it is the start of your time as a fully-fledged agent. I believe this is yours."

He offers you a piece of paper which you take from him. Lifting it up, you read what is written on it. "This certificate is awarded to certify the graduation of the trainee agent scheme and that the holder is now a qualified agent." Your eyes expand in disbelief at what you've just read. "A qualified agent" it didn't seem believable. You gaze up to D.O.C. so that he can confirm if this is true or not. He smiles back at you.

"Congratulations, and may I welcome you to the family. Welcome to the Anti-Bio Squad!"

Turn to page 90 to complete your graduation and claim your certificate!

8

You spend the rest of the flight in your own mind. The turbulence that plagued you before is completely irrelevant to you right now. You have the events of everything that has just happened, everything that's happened today, still replaying in your head over and over again. You somehow try to piece it all together to try to make sense of it. You know that none of that matters right now.

"You know, I was like you." Max projects his voice towards the aircraft's windscreen, where his vision is focused. "I was like you a couple of years ago when I was your age. I come from a family that nobody expected a lot from. All my brothers wanted to be footballers, but they knew they would just end up doing something else, something ordinary. I knew that couldn't be me. I knew of so many people who were getting sick and would ultimately get sicker because they weren't taking their anti-biotics properly. When I heard of the Anti-Bio Squad, and the work they were doing to put this right, I knew that I just had to do all I could to be a part of it."

His gaze is distracted for a second, looking down trying to hold a memory back from taking over his emotions too much. "I was so desperate to make a difference that at the start I used to get carried away trying help everyone. I put people in danger. But I now know I have to take cases seriously and to do things the right way. And you need to do that too. I know you can do it; I believe in you. You just need to take your time, think about it, be brave, and just get it right. We can't afford to let Jacob or anyone down. We need to get rid of these germs. Do you understand how important this is going to be?"

You understand.

The final hurdle is coming up, the make-or-break moment. If you're serious about being in The Anti-Bio Squad, and staying in the squad, then this had to go well.

You finally allow the outside world in just as the plane is on its descent into Jacob's mouth and has begun its shrinking function. You feel your heart start to race in your chest, unsure whether it is out of nerves or eagerness for the mission to go well. Once more, the plane times its flight perfectly, just as Jacob opens his mouth, and you fly between the two sets of teeth. The plane touches down in the centre of the tongue. Max calls the group together to prepare everyone for what's to come.

"Right, this is it. For some of you, this is your first time having a battle like this. Don't worry, we are all in this together and we are sticking with each other. Be smart out there, more importantly be safe." You look around the table and everyone has so much focus in their eyes. They are more than ready for the fight.

"We don't know how many of Strepto's clan is out there. It could potentially be millions of them. I imagine that they are going to come out at us quite hard. Again, keep yourselves safe. We will do our best to make sure everyone is covered, there's no need for anything silly to happen out there today. Which brings me to these, your Capsule Cannons." Max hands out the Capsule Cannons to the whole group.

"The Capsule Cannons will be your best friends today. Simple as anything: you point, the cannon fires, and mini tablets will be shot out. These tablets are vital as they contain the penicillin medicine that will keep these baddies down, stop the infection from spreading, and eventually get rid of it. Believe me, if we hit the

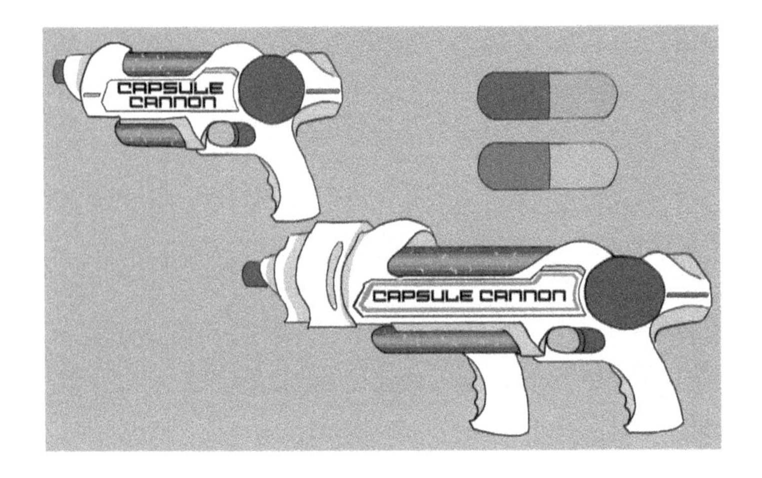

bacteria with a few of these, they will go down. Do not think that's your job done though, and this is the important part. They can get back up if they've only been hit by a small dosage. So, we need to do our best to make sure they stay down. We also need to make sure that we fire them down the throat at regular intervals, about every 4-6 hours for the next seven days so that it can get in the stomach and be absorbed into the blood stream. We do not leave here with any tablets left in these cannons." Max pauses for a moment. He takes a second to look everyone in the eye to make sure he still has their attention.

"I will say this again; WE DO NOT LEAVE HERE WITH ANY TABLETS LEFT IN THESE CANNONS. EVERYTHING WE HAVE BROUGHT

WITH US MUST BE USED. The tablets have been carefully measured out so that it is what is recommended for the *Streptococcus* bacteria that we are facing as well as right for little Jacob here. Now, is that understood?"

"Yes Agent Max." You join the other operatives with the collective, firm agreement.

"Well then. I'm not going to waste any more time. Let's get out there and show them why we are the Anti-Bio Squad!" The group roars to their feet in pumped excitement. Everyone grabs their own Capsule Cannon and heads straight out of the door down the steps of the plane.

No sooner has your head emerged from the plane, something flies past your vision, splattering on the side of the plane. Thick green mucus drips down onto your shoe. You try to flick the grossness off.

"It's started! Come on, let's look alive and get these bacteria!" The war cry bellows out from Max's lungs, echoing around Jacob's mouth.

Right in front of the plane is Strepto's clan. It's an army of bacteria willing and raring to cause damage and to infect people. Row after row is filled with large pea shaped germ soldiers, with arms and legs. Each soldier seems like they are a copy of the next. One of the *Streptococcus* germs from the centre makes a movement between a few of them. The one's closest appear to start fidgeting on the spot where they are standing. The first germ then retakes its original spot. It rolls its head back and unleashes an almighty roar. The sound echoes around the mouth and shivers down your spine making your hairs stand on edge. However, the roar proves to be a starter pistol for the clan as they all explode into action, beginning the barrage of the battle.

More mucus and pus balls are hurled into the air and surround you, some only missing you by millimetres. Each one that splatters next to you is another breath cut short as you begin to panic. You start to feel as though you have no place in this battle. You are helpless, glued to the top step of the plane's stairs.

"Newbie come on! Take cover with us, quick!" You head darts around trying to find the source of the yell. It is then that you realise that you are the only one remaining on the steps. Your eyes catch a hand calling you from down below you, Max is signalling you to join them. You dart down the steps, having to duck at any moment as more mucus rains down over your head. You turn out from the steps and are quickly dragged behind the plane's landing wheel to take cover with the rest of the group.

"Look guys, this is going to be even more difficult

than I thought." Max doing his best to bring control to the situation whilst still spluttering his words. Everyone seems frantic in trying to get their breath back. "It looks bad. There are a lot of them out there, but we can do this. We have no choice, Jacob needs us. We have got to dig down deep." He looks around the surrounding area to analyse the situation. For once, Max's eyes seem lost and empty of all ideas.

Max does one more sweep of everything in front of him, desperately trying to find an ember of hope that can spark The Anti-Bio Squad into life again. His pupils widen as an idea finally burns bright in his mind.

"Right, I've got it. What we are going to do is you, operatives, you advance forward to make a sweeping line at the end of the plane. Newbie and I will cover you from back here until you get into position. From there, you should be able to build a solid base to pick off a large bulk of them. You guys will then be the cover for us as we are going to swing round the back and, using the teeth as a line of cover, we are going to try and hit them from multiple directions. After that, Newbie is going to hold position there and then I'll get to the back of the mouth and I'll just unload whatever's left in my Capsule Cannon straight down the throat. The quicker that we can get this medicine into Jacob's system the weaker these guys will be and so the easier they will be to fend off. So, if we are all in understanding then let's make the move on three, okay? Right, ready. 1… 2… 3!"

The operatives fling themselves forward, straight into an airspace of flying mucus balls. Max rises to his feet and, in a tall strong stance, starts firing at will in the direction of the clan. He is making contact with a germ soldier with every shot fired, firing like poetry in motion. You pull your legs up to be brave and join Max at his side. However, your inexperience shows being right next to a veteran like Max. You fire the odd tablet from time to time and when you are able to get a tablet away it more than often misses the target. You look out though, and the *Streptococcus* seem like they are being contained. A small number of the soldiers have already fallen, and the air strikes of mucus are less frequent. Instead, the germs are visibly jolting from side to side trying to avoid being hit by a tablet.

"STAGE TWO!" Max strains to make his voice heard above the battle. "Newbie, follow me."

It is now your turn to move frantically. The majority of the clan is distracted with the rest of the battle but enough are noticing you flee to another covering spot and once more fill the area with pus balls. You are forced to hop from side to side, zig-zagging the onslaught. Your determination pushes your feet onwards, each step, each stride, each hop making you gain in speed and gain confidence.

Your confidence is short lived. You become so focused about continuing forward and making it to the safe spot that you nearly get hit by three pus balls in quick succession. The first one flies over and only becomes visible in the corner of your eye. Out of instinct or maybe luck you stop dead in your stride as the missile lands right in front of you and the gunk squirts down the front of your legs. Before you can even act grossed out by the pus, the next two soon follow and land again at your feet.

Luckily, Penny is right there for you. She grabs your arm in her mouth and yanks you over to the nearest tooth and guides you around the corner to safety. You fall to your bum, panting desperately to try and get some more air into your lungs; the pus attack scare has taken a lot of the wind out of you and very nearly took more than that. You feel you owe it to Penny to give her a quick tickle under the chin. Amongst it all, Max has jumped around to join you both.

"Nice save, Penny! You wouldn't believe how many times she's saved me. Yes, you have, who's a good girl?

Right okay, Newbie? You can take a quick breather, but it really has to be a quick one because we are still in a battle here. This isn't quite where I wanted us to be positioned but it will still work fine. This is important now; I need you to be my cover so I can go to the back of the mouth and get these tablets down the throat in his system as soon as possible. I believe in you; I know you can do it."

You hoist yourself to your feet using the tooth as an aid to help you up. Max's words inspire you to psych yourself up and be at your best for rest of the mission. The operatives need you. Max needs you. Jacob needs you.

"Okay, I'm going to make my move on the count of three. Ready? 1… 2… 3!" Max makes his desperate dash from behind the tooth right through the middle of the action. Even knowing about the move, you find yourself surprised by Max's daring nature. You do your best Max impression and stand tall behind the tooth, beginning your fire on the bacteria to try and clear a path for Max.

You aim is still shaky and misses more targets than ones that you hit. You try your best to steady yourself, even resting the cannon on the top of the molar as support but you soon realise that it is your hand and your trigger finger that is doing the majority of the shaking. Luckily, Max proves himself to be the skilled agent that he is and manages to take out the majority of the targets in his way. You do your best to assist Max with the few that remain in front of him.

SPLAT!

A pus ball drops on the tooth directly in front of you and sends splatter in all directions including your face. Your vision becomes blurred, and you soon drop to the ground. Thankfully, you easily wipe away all of the gunk using your shirt; however, the close encounter again has left you breathless. You close your eyes in dread, thinking about what would have happened if it was a direct hit. You spend a few moments taking in long, deep breaths attempting to steady your racing heart, caught up in the fast-paced battle.

You are clueless as to how you've managed to force yourself to do it but remarkedly you drag yourself off the floor to peer over the tooth once more. This time you refrain from making yourself too visible whilst your eyes dart around the area looking for anything – good or bad. You are alarmed to see Max is nowhere in sight. You have complete faith and trust that Max would be okay on his own, that he is more than skilled enough to make it through without your cover, however you can't help but to begin to panic that the worst may have happened.

A sickness lines the pit of your stomach thinking about losing Max and it being all your fault. You try to push the fear out of your mind and to take charge of the situation again. You are desperate to be a part of the action, but you struggle to force your body out from behind the tooth wall. Instead, you remain where you are positioned and try to help the operatives clear the battlefield. All you are successful in doing is adding three more germs to the many that the operatives have managed to take down. Each shot is delayed by another guilty thought about risking Max's life. You try to keep the faith that Max is fine and is trying to save the mission, but with every second that passes a glimmer of the faith dwindles.

The remaining clan members advance forward, more ferocious than previously. They start to stack on top of each other to form a chain of bacteria, trying to enforce themselves and make them stronger in the attack. You sense that they want to seek revenge for their fallen comrades. With every moment that passes without any sign of Max an extra beat is added to the rhythm of your heart. He's got to be okay. He's been doing this for years and must have faced a lot worse than this. He's faced a lot worse than this on almost a daily basis. This is surely quite a straightforward mission procedure for him. He could do the mission with his eyes closed without falling into any bit of danger. Surely this is going to be another successful mission to add to his collection. Surely?

Whether it is the desperation of trying to find Max or the guilt of feeling you should be doing more in the battle, you decide to move. Jumping one tooth at a time, maintaining your cover all the while, you move three teeth across. You hope that the fresh angle will reveal the sight you were hoping for. Nothing. The thumping in your chest is quickening. You hope Max is okay.

Still nothing can be seen. You decide to dart back to the tooth you were hiding behind in the first place and then shift over once more but in the opposite direction this time. Another new angle. Another one with no luck. The beat has intensified now. Any moment you feel like it's going to burst inside of you. Come on, Max!

You look over to see even the operatives break their line of defence. For every few paces the germs advance forward, the operatives shuffle back a step trying to keep their distance. The *Streptococcus* bacteria still have the numbers on you all and now have the determination. You run around the back of the teeth, moving further down towards the operatives to join them in their defence.

The bacteria can't be more than 10 metres away now, with each advancement you start to dread what would happen to you as a result of a full-blown bacteria attack. Then, without warning, one from in the middle of the advancing bacteria line falls forward, dropping to the ground. It's Max. He appears in the middle and instantly picks off two more of the bacteria.

The *Streptococcus* bacteria turn away from you reacting to three of their own suddenly falling. Their confusion about an attack from the back provides the perfect opportunity for the operatives to pick off the last remaining clan members. As the final one drops to the ground, silence falls upon the battlefield for the first time.

"Wow, that was a close one!" Wiping a bead of sweat

off his brow, Max blows out a gust of air. "I normally save a small number of tablets for the end just in case, and thankfully I did this time."

The operatives chuckle with Max, although you can sense that there is a huge amount of relief with each chuckle.

"Right, I am all out of tablets so if you guys are then I think it's time we got out of here!" All the operatives mutter in agreeance with Max once they have checked their cannons over. They gingerly start the plod back to the safety of the plane.

"Well, what a first mission this has been for you Newbie. D.O.C. definitely didn't pick an easy one for you to start with but in the end that didn't matter. We've done it! You've done it. We will have to come back a few more times just to carry on the dosage but right now, we can go back and celebrate your first mission! I'm so proud of you." Max slaps you on the back and offers you a beaming smile before he bounds up the steps to the plane.

You go to plant your foot on the first step, but it slips on a small slimy mucus puddle. Your Capsule Cannon slips from your hands and falls to the ground. Bending over to pick up, you notice a number on the side of the cannon: '10% of ammunition remaining'.

You had completely neglected to look at how much ammunition you had left and it's clear that you have more still to use. You look up at the top of the steps. Max is no longer there; he has joined everybody else on the plane and are all ready to head back to The Lab. You consider whether to fire the rest of the tablets, or whether to give in to your tiredness and to not keep everyone waiting anymore and just head back to The Lab.

It's your choice what you think you should do next:

If you think you have done enough with the mission and so will take the remaining tablets back to the base as spare, then turn to page 82.

Or, if you think you ought to carry on and use all of the antibiotic ammunition that's left, then turn to page 48.

7b

You stare, motionless, at the flashing button for a couple of seconds. Like a moth to a bright light, your finger is drawn to the button until you feel the contact made with the tablet's glass screen. You know there is no turning back now, so you release the pressure under your finger, releasing the penicillin antibiotics to Georgie at the same time too. She must have needed the help, or she wouldn't have asked, right?

You hear the familiar echoing of footsteps running up the corridor.

"Newbie! They are loading the plane. We need to get moving right now. Come on, follow me." Here you go again. He grabs the tablet from your hand and then grabs your other hand dragging you up the corridor with him.

There's a frantic buzz bouncing its way between everyone on the plane. You are sat with Max in the cockpit as before but now joining you in the main compartment of the plane are five operatives.

"It's always easier having a little helping hand in situations like this. We really do go into it blind; we have no idea how many of Strepto's clan is going to be there, so we need the operatives as back up. We will still use the same dosage of penicillin against the *Streptococcus*, we must ensure that we spread out the doses amongst us all so we can deliver regular doses 4 times a day for the next 7 days, we MUST give Jacob the full course of antibiotics or Empress Strepto will grow resistant to the drugs and then we will have nothing to fight her with. She will win, and children will get very poorly from the infections because of it. I don't even want to think of that as a possibility. The first time is always the hardest, but we get it right then we can leave the back up here to carry on with the regular dosages in shifts."

Your head turns away from Max, looking out to the empty sky outside the window. You hope that your eyes don't give you away about how nervous you are for your first battle. It's the right thing, it needs to be done and this is exactly what you signed up for, but these thoughts don't do anything to settle the butterflies in your stomach.

"INCOMING MESSAGE ALERT!" The already

too familiar warning rings out on the speaker in the cockpit. "Receiving message from the D.O.C., do you accept?" He must be checking on you both and wishing you luck ahead of the mission.

"Agent Max accepting message."

"Max! Do you know what's happened? Where are you right now?" D.O.C.'s voice is still somehow as intimidating even without seeing his face to accompany the message. However, you are quite relieved that you can't see him as you get the impression he isn't in the mood for jokes at the moment.

"Uhmm… well we… me and Newbie that is. We are just on one of the planes heading to Jacob to start the treatment process and…"

"Well, do you know what's happened?" The D.O.C.'s yell cuts off Max in tracks. "Do you know what that Newbie has done?" Max shoots you with a look. Clearly, he didn't know what it was that you were supposed to have done – and more importantly, neither did you.

"Georgie sent out a distress message asking if she could use some of your penicillin tablets for her mission, and Newbie has only gone and sent them to her!" You face starts to burn red as you slide back into the chair. "And Newbie knows you're not supposed to share antibiotics, I've said about the specialties and you have said as well. Thank goodness, it was all staged, I was trying to test Newbie. Safe to say, it was a resounding fail!" Your body fills to the tips with regret and guilt. How could you have forgotten to mention it? How could you have been so naïve with your decision?

"This does not happen again, no more slip ups. If this mission doesn't go smoothly, Newbie's gone. I don't care. There's too much at stake. And you can tell Newbie however you like, as long as the message is understood." The sound cuts out.

The two of you sit there still and silent. The buzz fizzled out of the room. You can't even bring yourself to look at Max. Your head hangs down with D.O.C.'s harsh words still echoing around your ears. Finally, Max leans over to break the silence.

"I'm sorry you had to hear that. I get it, you made a mistake and it's not good, but you shouldn't have had to hear that." His hand consoles your shoulder. "But he's right though. This is a great job but it's such a dangerous and difficult one. The choices we make really are huge. They make such an enormous difference on somebody being ill or not. Sharing antibiotics can result in the mistreatment of infections and in bacteria gaining resistance to antibiotics. Not only that but, you could have given the bacteria multi-antibiotic resistance and then in the future none of our antibiotics would work. I can't stress this enough, but children could get extremely poorly from simple infections. That's why we have to do all we can to make sure we make the right decision." He looks you up and down, knowing that each word was making very little difference in changing your mood.

"Hey, look at me. You're not a bad trainee. You're not a bad agent. You've done so well so far, keeping up with it all, I've been so impressed. What's happened has happened. We can't change that. But we can change things for this little boy Jacob. Let's have a good mission, let's hit these pesky *Streptococcus* bacteria with everything we've got, and let's help Jacob get back to feeling well soon again. Come on, we can do this". You reluctantly nod your head back at him. You hope that Max is right.

Turn to page 53 to continue to the next stage of the case.

6

"Well, there's no rest for the wicked here. It's time to get stuck into work again." Max accompanies the line with a hearty slap on your back, but it's still not to jolt you into action again. You stand there with your hands held at the back of your head. You are still trying to catch your breath and process everything that has just happened. "We've just found the bad guys, now the real fun starts trying to take care of them!" Gently slapping the cheek of your face, you manage to snap yourself out of it and regain your focus again.

"So, what's going to happen now is we are going to fly back down into the boy's mouth – sorry about that but there's no other way – and it's going to be a battle with those bacteria. And if there's going to be a battle, we are going to need backup and we are going to need antibiotic ammunition to treat the boy and wipe out the *Streptococcus*, so they don't come back. I'm going to sort out all of that now, you just wait here though. You look like you could do with a couple of minutes." Max darts off, down one of the corridors before you have a chance to even give a reply. You did need the break though.

You couldn't have taken more than a few breaths before you feel a vibration coming from your backpack. Swinging the bag round your shoulder, you pull the zip down to retrieve the tablet device, forgetting that Max had left it with you. The screen is flashing with bright red letters 'Incoming Message'.

"Hey Max, I really need your help wi-oh, Newbie. It's you. Listen, is Max around?" It's Georgie, with an unusual sense of urgency in her voice. You compose yourself before delivering your reply. "Stay out there

and hold your position! We've got to hold them off. Never mind, Newbie, there's no time. I need you. The other mission that D.O.C. sent me on has turned nasty really quickly. It's a poor girl from the South-East called Mariah, she's only 5. They are draining us for everything we've got. I wouldn't normally ask this, but can you send in some of your antibiotic supplies?"

The request catches you off guard. It's still your first day on the job as a trainee and not only have you lead an investigation on a bacterial crime, one of the top agents has come to you in dire need of your help. Is this really happening? It is only then that you remember the conversations you had earlier, about specialties, about specific teams, and equipment for specific bacterial infections. You share your concern with Georgie.

"You're quite right, and we might be okay with what we have. I am worried though that we might be overpowered, and this poor girl is going to get sicker. I'll send you the file over, so you can have a read before deciding what to do. Whatever you choose is fine, I get it, but just make it quick! Please."

The file pops up on the tablet. It sparks a million questions in your mind. Is this right? What would Max do? What would D.O.C. think if it's the wrong choice? Is this all really happening? It is happening, and you know you need to make something happen now. In the corner of the screen, a button flashes asking you to 'Send Help?'.

What action should you take?

Try to help Georgie by sending her your penicillin tablets, turn to page 69.

Or, choose not to send Georgie your penicillin tablets, turn to page 38.

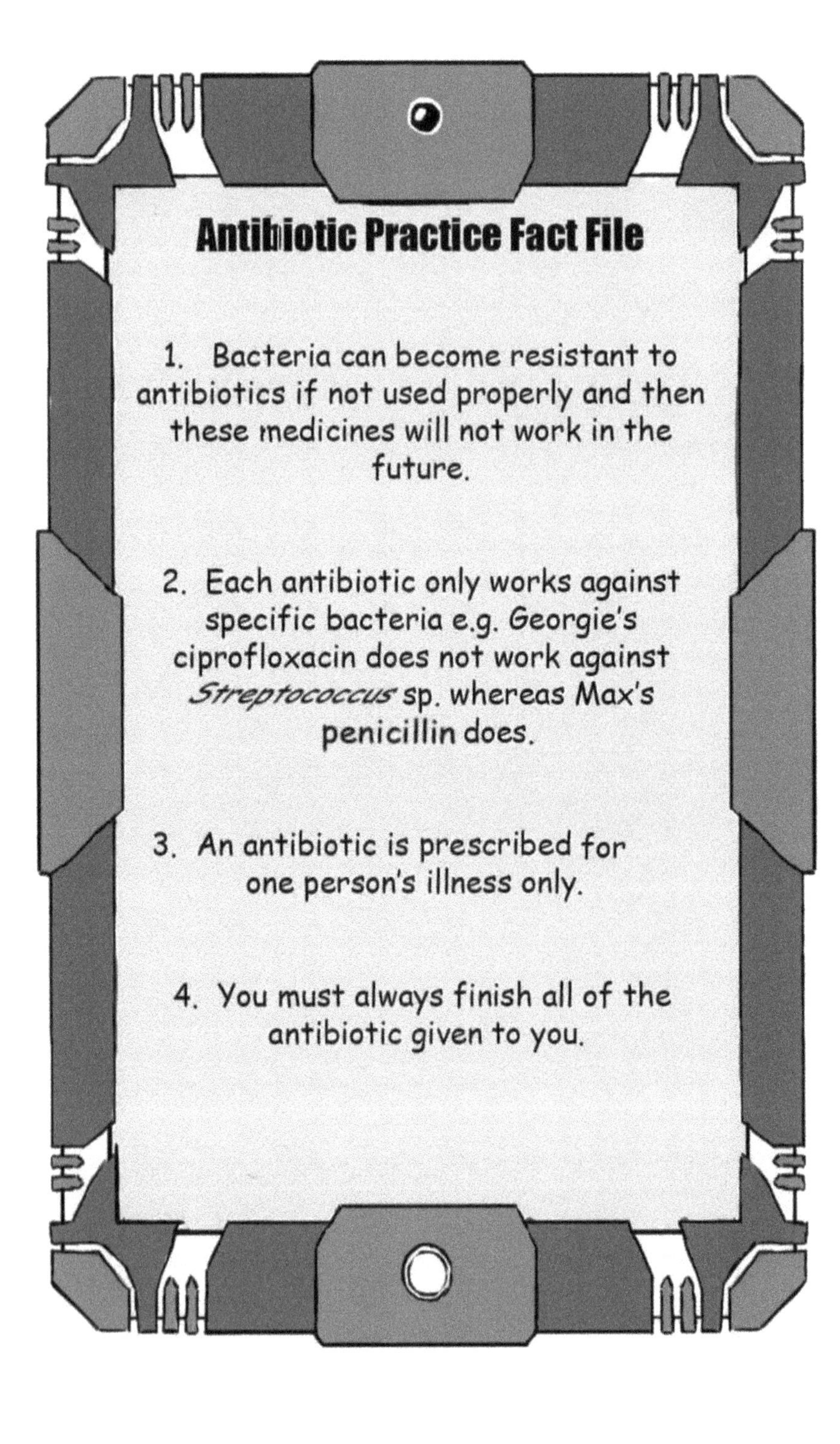
Antibiotic Practice Fact File
1. Bacteria can become resistant to antibiotics if not used properly and then these medicines will not work in the future.
2. Each antibiotic only works against specific bacteria e.g. Georgie's ciprofloxacin does not work against Streptococcus sp. whereas Max's penicillin does.
3. An antibiotic is prescribed for one person's illness only.
4. You must always finish all of the antibiotic given to you.

5b

You review the files of both gangs thoroughly, staring down at the screen hoping that something would pop out and make the decision for you. The images and words just become blurs and blobs as the pressure builds and you stop being able to take in the information. You stop yourself, eyes closed, and draw a deep breath in. You've made your decision.

"You think it's Strepto? Are you sure?" You nod your head back at Max, albeit cautiously as you are far from confident about making a decision like this. "Right then, that's a very brave decision. But let's go for it." The two of you take off, running straight up the steps to the plane, and fly off back out of the mouth.

*

It feels like you haven't stopped rushing as you burst through each set of doors in the corridors of The Lab. You follow closely behind Max, trying your best to stick to his pace and also trying to follow his direction so that you do not get lost in the labyrinth. You find your way to the centre control room.

"Right." Taking a moment so he can catch his breath. "We need to call this into D.O.C. so we can get the all clear. Computer, transmit message to the D.O.C." The pair of you twitch as you wait for the call to connect.

"D.O.C. here. What's wrong, Max? What do you have to tell me?" Max turns his head to face you, double checking that this is still the decision you want to go with.

"We checked out the case you sent us on, about the boy with cold symptoms, and we investigated and discussed the situation and we've decided to diagnose it as a case of bacterial *Streptococcus* in the throat. We did also find evidence of the Rhinos being in Jacob's throat which has paved the way for Empress Strepto but we just needed to get the okay from you."

"Did you make the decision, or did you do as I said and allow Newbie to make it?"

"It was all Newbie." You both stand there facing the screen, for what feels like an eternity, waiting for D.O.C. to pass his judgement. The silence becomes deafening and adds to the already uncomfortable situation.

It crosses your mind that the connection may have dropped and he might be frozen on screen. However, you notice the slightest twitch of movement. Below his moustache, the corners of a smile creeps out.

"Good work, Newbie. You made a good call. Now go out there and get Strepto's clan of no-goods. Keep me posted." The call drops as does your posture, not realising how straight and stiff you were holding yourself.

"You did it! Get in, I'm so happy for you." You are swallowed into Max's arms for a big hug. "We can't celebrate yet though. There's still plenty of work still to be done. But after pulling off that decision, I think we've got this. Good job!"

Turn to page 74 to find out what's next in the investigation.

9a

You stand there, hovering on the spot for a few moments. You feel so drained and empty. You are battle worn. The past day has more than taken its toll. Your eyes nearly fall out of your head when you realise that this is still your first day in the Anti-Bio Squad. No way has this been just one day. You let out a big deep sigh as your foot drops to a step-in front and you follow all the way up the steps and into the plane.

You are greeted by a wave of cheering and whooping from everyone on board the plane. Everyone is overjoyed at the "job well done" that they've achieved. A wave of high fives and pats on the back more than encourages you that you have made the right career path and that you now feel like one of the team. Imagine that, a part of the famous Anti-Bio Squad. When the cheering dies down, you wander over to a seat away from everyone in the middle of the plane.

This has been a test like no other you have experienced. The whole adventure has pushed you to a limit you didn't know you had. However, sitting in the comfy leather on the plane, you feel your heart rate slowly return to a regular beat. Your eyelids begin to feel like they are magnetised as they draw closer and closer together until you can't fight it any longer and allow yourself to rest and close your eyes.

*

The clunking of the plane steps on the concrete floor wakes you from your nap. Your eyelids still feel heavy and your head is still overloaded with the memory of all of today's events, but you do feel the rest has done at least a little bit of good for you. Afterall, you need to be refreshed for the celebratory party that is about to happen for your first successful mission.

You look out of the plane window, expecting to see a crowd of people welcoming you back from your triumphant mission. However, you are left disappointed at the sight of an empty hangar. You don't allow this to ruin your mood though. Everyone is still working in HQ and are waiting to throw the party there. You rise out of your seat, noticing that there is nobody left on the plane. You assume that they all saw that you were sleeping and chose to leave you resting. Upon exiting, you turn around to face the plane. You feel a proud smirk come over you as you relive the success of your mission.

You follow the long corridor leading to the main control room from the hangar and you mind starts to go giddy, teasing what the celebration is going to be like when you get there. They would probably get a massive cake to celebrate in your honour, or they might organise a disco party to end the celebratory occasion. Surely no trainee has ever taken on a mission as grand as yours on their very first day, and you felt quietly confident that none of them would have done as well on the mission as you have. Your reward is bound to be an enormous gesture.

Approaching the doors to the control room, you can hear very little or next to no noise coming from within. You chuckle to yourself realising they had gone for the surprise party approach. Not wanting to spoil the surprise, you try to compose yourself and act surprise but you're not able to remove your beaming smile. To not delay things any further, you enter the room.

You are presented with a very normal control room where everyone is very focused on the job in hand, exactly the same as how you left the place earlier. The lack of a party forces you to raise an eyebrow but you do consider that everyone is still working and so you decide that they are waiting to have the party later when everyone is finished working. You walk to the centre of the headquarters to get a better viewpoint.

Max enters the room and you both spot each other at the same time. You can't help but to wear a great grin on your face once more as he approaches you purposefully.

"You need to come with me." Max mutters the words to you with a stern expression. It leaves you feeling quite uncertain about where you're going and what you're needed for. The pair of you leave the control room and turn into the first available interview room. Max offers you a chair, which you take, and you look up to see D.O.C. already shown on the screen. He lets out a deep sigh.

"Well Newbie, I am not going to beat around the bush, I am just going to come out and say it. Whilst you were sleeping on the plane, we did our routine clear down of the plane and equipment, and we did a debrief about the mission. Doing this, we discovered that one of the Capsule Cannons still contained antibiotic ammunition."

You heart sinks into the very pit of your body. You

know exactly where this conversation is going and you're not going to enjoy it.

"That Capsule Cannon was yours from the mission. Not only have you defied Max's orders as your superior, not only have you defied my orders as the director of this whole programme, but you have also put a poor child's health at risk. I thought I made it clear that it is vital that we have to get the dosages absolutely right on our missions. If we don't do our job right with the antibiotics, then it can lead to Jacob not being able to clear the bacteria out of his system, making him ill for longer or getting a worse illness and giving Empress Strepto and her clan resistance to our penicillin tablets. Your actions today have put a child's health at risk and that is simply unacceptable here. I hope you realise that. What do you have to say for yourself?"

You sit there with nothing to say. You knew you were taking a risk by not emptying the rest of the cannon, but you were too focused on being tired to do something about it. Your selfish act has now made a boy sicker than he already was and you've allowed Empress Strepto to become stronger. You are the only one to blame for it. From deep in your stomach, the guilt builds and builds and builds making you feel even more sick than facing turbulence on the planes. You are helpless but to sit there with your head low and to take your punishment.

"I liked you, kid. I really did." The disappointment in the D.O.C.'s voice makes every word feel like another blow to your stomach. "The whole reason you were selected is because we had great expectations of you and, unfortunately, you have let me down. You've let us all down. Other mistakes can be excused and forgotten but this was unacceptable."

You feel it coming, the D.O.C.'s very last blow. The knockout punch. You can sense it coming but you still dread it.

"I am so sorry, but I don't see you as a part of the programme anymore. You're not Anti-Bio Squad material. So, you can consider this trainee programme cancelled until you are able and willing to try again some other time. But right now, you're done. Goodbye."

Sadly, you weren't able to graduate into the Anti-Bio Squad this time. However, you can turn the page to read the helpful germ guide or turn back to the start to the start to try again and do your bit in the Fight Against Resistance.

The Anti-Bio Squad Germ Guide

Antibiotics are important in helping to make you better, but bacteria can become resistant to the medicine and then they won't cure you in the future.

As an Anti-Bio Squad Agent, it is your job to remember the following facts:

- **Do not** use antibiotics for a cold (it is a virus not a bacteria), you will be helping Empresses Strepto and other bad bacteria become stronger.
- **Do not** share antibiotics with anyone, they are for your use ONLY!
- **Always** listen to the Doc. or other healthcare practitioners (Pharmacists and Nurses). They are the experts on when to use antibiotics, how much to use, and for how long.
- **Always** finish the course of antibiotics, if you don't the bacteria will become stronger.

It's all up to you now. You are ready! As the newest trained Anti-Bio Squad Agent, it's up to you to fight the cause and encourage others to do the same. Teach everyone about how to be antibiotic aware so they too can become agents. It is only working together that will help us beat this battle. Together we will win this fight, the 'Fight Against Resistance!'

Congratulations once again for completing the mission successfully! You are now a full member of the Anti-Bio Squad. Help your friends and family by using the helpful 'Germ Guide' so they can be equipped and ready to battle bacteria and help win the Fight Against Resistance!

To download your Anti-Bio Squad certificate, go to www.germsjourney.com or scan the QR code. You can also follow the link to find out more online.

A Germ's Journey

Follow the journey of a germ from the toilet seat to the tummy (and out again!) Using unique heat-sensitive pages, colourful illustrations and a parent/teacher guide, explore the concepts of germ transfer and the importance of handwashing with young children!

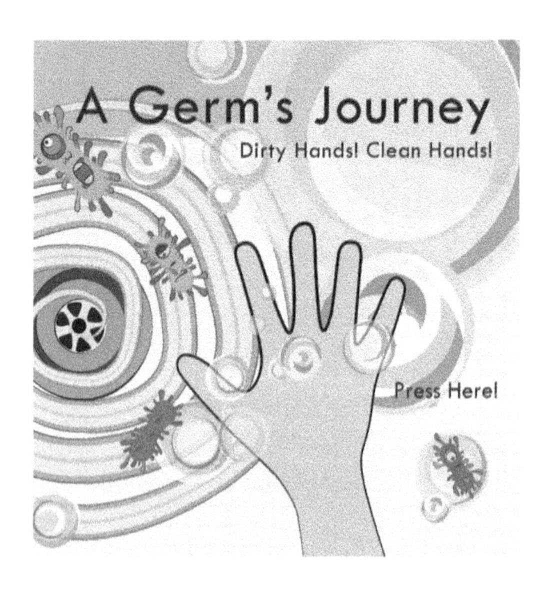

Bye Bye Germs!

Jess and her brother Joe were playing with their toys when Jess felt a tickle in her throat. The little tickle turned into a bigger tickle. And the bigger tickle turned into a giant cough and sneeze! Can they stop the germs from spreading? Join them on their journey and learn how to become a handwashing superhero!

Bye-Bye Germs includes fact boxes to inform both children and parents/carers of the science behind the story.

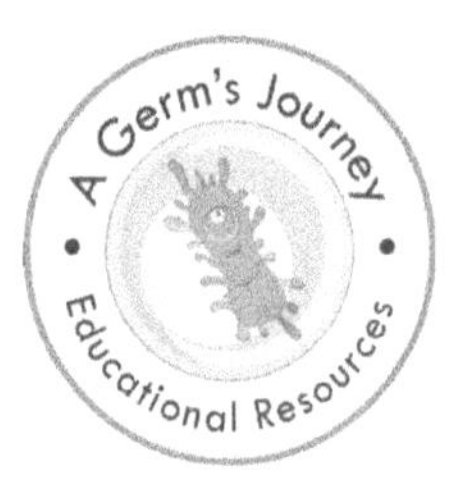

More information about the books is available at www.germsjourney.com or www.medinapublishing.com

Matador